Little Pig Is Capable

For Kale, always capable,
and little Stella, capable too

www.houghtonmifflinbooks.com

The text of this book is set in Frutiger Bold.
The illustrations are gouache.

Library of Congress Cataloging-in-Publication Data

Roche, Denis (Denis M.)
Little Pig is capable / by Denis Roche.
p.   cm.
Summary: Little Pig's parents worry about him so much that it's embarrassing,
but all their warnings come in handy when he goes on a hike with his Snout
Scout troop and their strange substitute troop leader.
ISBN 0-395-91368-3
[1. Pigs—Fiction. 2. Wolves—Fiction. 3. Scouts and scouting—Fiction.] I. Title.
PZ7.R5843 Li 2002
[E]—dc21
2001016583

Printed in Singapore
TWP 10 9 8 7 6 5 4 3 2 1

Little Pig Is Capable

Denis Roche

Houghton Mifflin Company

Boston 2002

Little Pig's parents worried about him all the time.

They fussed,

"Honey-bunches, don't ever stand up in the bathtub. If you do, you could fall and break your tail, the ambulance will come, and the neighbors will wonder, all before you've washed behind your ears."

they fretted,

and they embarrassed him to no end.

They treat me like a baby, thought Little Pig. He wondered if his parents would ever stop worrying.

"Precious Piggy-Wiggy, on a day like this the sun will be hot, and if you're not protected, you could burn to a crisp, your skin will turn red and then purple, you'll swell up like a balloon, and you'll be in terrible, terrible pain."

One sunny Saturday, Little Pig's Snout Scout troop was going on a hike up a nearby mountain. Ma and Pop Pig helped Little Pig get dressed. They pulled a big floppy hat onto his head, smeared sunscreen on his snout, and covered his eyes with enormous sunglasses.

"I can dress myself," said Little Pig, but his parents weren't done yet.

"Sweetie-pie, this time of year the mosquitoes are the size of birds. One bite and you'll be sooo sorry! Always wear your water wings around water, and don't go swimming if the water is rough! Remember your cousin Ricky—he got swept away and was never heard from again. Now mind that your shoelaces don't come undone."

Ma and Pop Pig tucked Little Pig's pants into his socks, slipped water wings onto his arms, and laced his feet into sturdy boots.

"I'll be fine," said Little Pig, and he didn't even have to look in the mirror to know how ridiculous he looked.

"Dearest Piggy-treasure, we made you twenty-two beet and onion sandwiches so you could keep your strength up throughout the day. Don't drink your eggplant-banana juice all at once. Take sips whenever you feel thirsty! If you don't stay hydrated, you'll overheat, your brain will melt, and you'll shrivel up like a prune."

Ma and Pop Pig packed a knapsack full of sandwiches and a canteen full of juice and drove Little Pig to the base of the mountain where the Snout Scouts were meeting.

Bob Swine, the usual troop leader, was absent.

"I'm Ravenous," said a lean pig in sunglasses, "the substitute." He shook hands with Ma and Pop Pig while Little Pig got in line with the rest of the scouts.

As Little Pig hiked away, Ma and Pop Pig thought of one more thing to worry about.

"Be wary of wolves!" they called.

But Little Pig was being teased by the other Snout Scouts and didn't hear them.

The path was steep, and within minutes the Snout Scouts were thinking about lunch. "Is it time to eat yet?" they asked.

"Be full!" said Ravenous, and all the scouts, except Little Pig, finished their lunches.

Now, without the weight of their food, the Snout Scouts moved faster up the mountain. Soon they were very, very thirsty.

"Can we drink our juice?" they asked.

"Be moist!" said Ravenous, and the scouts, except Little Pig, polished off their juice, leaving none for later.

Up, up, up the mountain went the Snout Scouts. The day was hot, getting hotter, and when the scouts came upon a roaring stream, they squealed with delight.

"Can we swim?" they asked.

"Be clean!" said Ravenous, and he filed his nails as everybody, except Little Pig, struggled to swim in the strong currents.

When the Snout Scouts crawled out of the water, they fell asleep in the sun.

"They're going to get burned," said Little Pig, who knew that their sunscreen had washed off in the water.

"They'll be perfectly crispy!" said Ravenous, rubbing his stomach.

Little Pig ate another sandwich in the shade. When he saw Ravenous licking his lips, Little Pig offered him one.

"Appetizer!" said Ravenous, and he greedily ate the twenty beet and onion sandwiches left.

There's something not so nice about Ravenous, thought Little Pig.

Eventually the Snout Scouts woke up. They were dizzy with sunburn, hunger, and thirst, and they couldn't be bothered to put on their boots and socks.

"Let's go home," said Ravenous, and soon everybody, except for Little Pig, had blistery feet.

Only Little Pig noticed that they were heading *up* the mountain, not down.
He became suspicious.

When the path turned into the forest, the mosquitoes got fierce.

"We're getting bitten by bugs," complained the Snout Scouts.

"Dinnertime!" cried Ravenous. He ordered the bug-bitten, blistery, dizzy, sunburned, thirsty, hungry Snout Scouts to collect wood for a fire.

Only Little Pig remembered that there was no food left to eat.
Now he grew more suspicious.

Ravenous was having a difficult time trying to light a fire. He took off his hat and sunglasses so he could see better.

Suddenly Little Pig realized who Ravenous was. Ravenous was
a WOLF and the Snout Scouts were going to be his dinner!
Little Pig had to save the Snout Scouts!

Watching Ravenous, Little Pig had an idea.
"That magnifying glass will work better," he said, "if you hold it right up to the sun."

Ravenous held up the magnifying glass and foolishly looked through it at the sun.
   "I can't see!" he howled. Little Pig was ready. In a jiffy Ravenous was handcuffed, muzzled, and harmless.

Little Pig revived the Snout Scouts with eggplant-banana juice and gave them their missing boots and socks.

Then, holding Ravenous tightly by the tail, he led everybody back down the mountain.

When they heard how Little Pig had saved the Snout Scout troop,
Ma and Pop Pig beamed with pride.

"Our Little Pig!" said Ma Pig, hugging him hard.

"Our capable pig!" said Pop Pig, hugging him harder.

From that day on, Little Pig was called Capable Pig, and his parents never, ever worried about him.

Well, almost never.